My mother-in-law, Svitlana, for answering all my questions and checking my Russian.

Nichole Chase, for... well, you know.

Patricia Eddy for being the most badass editor under a deadline. I love you.

*And certainly not least, to my **Secret Proofreading Ninjas:** Brittany, Lauren, Maria, Kate, Andrea, Jami, Allison, Samantha, Dani, Oksana, and Marianne. You made this happen.*

KARPOV KINRADE

FOREVER BOUND

VAMPIRE BRIDES

ISBN-13: 978-1-939559-57-9

CHAPTER 1: OTHERWISE KNOWN AS THAT TIME I MADE THE WRONG LIFE CHOICE AND ENDED UP A HUMAN SACRIFICE

WHY AM I tied to a tree in the middle of a freezing Ukrainian forest waiting for a god to come devour me?

Funny story.

Let me start at the beginning. I'm Evangeline Love. Yes, I know, it's the corniest name in the history of names, but it's mine and I love it...pun always intended. My friends just call me Angel. Or Love. Depends on how long we've been friends.

This is my last year of grad school. I'm nearly done with my thesis and will soon be a practicing Marriage and Family Therapist in the Greater Los Angeles area.

All my dreams are about to come true.

So how did I wind up in my current predicament, so far from the concrete jungle of Los Angeles, where my biggest problem was rush hour traffic?

Because I made the wrong life choice a few months ago when I agreed to join my Ukrainian roommate for a trip to her homeland for the holidays. She and I have been through a lot together since the night we met as freshmen, equal measures scared and excited, but I've never seen where she's from, and this seemed like a good time. I have no family and no significant other with claims to my Christmas, so this was a welcome invite, and I've been anticipating this trip with excitement for months. I was packed before Thanksgiving.

In the understatement of the year, I didn't anticipate the fate that has befallen me.

Yana and I left LAX at two in the morning for an exhausting sixteen-hour flight with one layover.

We were at the tail end of our journey and both asleep when the plane began to jerk in the sky in ways you really don't want the shit ton of steel you're flying through the air in to do.

The voice of the pilot came on to warn us that we were experiencing turbulence.

No shit.

We were over Ukraine at the time. So close to our final destination.

Yana woke, her seafoam-colored eyes wide with alarm.

I reached for her hand as the emergency air bags dropped from above us, and a flight attendant gave instructions in English, Ukrainian, and Russian. I couldn't hear her though.

Because the plane was dropping from the sky at an alarming rate.

We were going to crash. I knew it in my bones.

Yana and I both closed our eyes and gripped each other with everything in us as the air pressure in the cabin changed and the plane began to tailspin mid-air.

The rest comes to me in flashes.

Screaming.

Blood.

Hanging upside down from the seat belt.

Purses and laptops flying through the cabin.

More screaming.

A child crying.

The same child tragically going silent.

A parent sobbing.

Panic flooding me.

I couldn't think past the shock of falling from the sky.

None of us would survive. We were all doomed.

And then.

Nothing.

I remember nothing after that moment until I woke up tied to this tree, freezing my ass off in the middle of a forest.

It was light when I first woke, though the sun had just begun to set. I was gagged and hanging limply from my restraints. Rope dug into the exposed flesh of my arms, wrists, and legs. My lips were pulled into a grotesque joker smile by the cloth shoved into my mouth and tied around my head, and something viscous dripped into my eyes, stinging them.

Given the pounding headache that had me nearly in tears, my guess was blood.

And when I tried to wiggle out of the restraints, I felt every cut, bruise and strain that falling seven miles in an airplane would inevitably cause. I pushed through the pain, struggling more fiercely, but not only did I make no progress in loosening the ropes, I rather unfortunately caught the attention of whom I suspected was the dude in charge.

Which is when it fully registered that I wasn't alone.

The man standing before me was dressed in a similar fashion to the other men gathered, if not a little fancier. He wore dark baggy pants, a white shirt with intricate red embroidery that Yana had told me is an important tradition and art in Ukrainian culture, an embroidered vest, and a thick sash with fringed edges around his waist. His steel grey eyes were hard and his face impassive as he stared at me. He looked to be in his mid-60s and clearly commanded respect amongst the other villagers, who waited to see what he would do now that I was awake.

As details around me came into focus, the music that had drifted into my subconscious while I was passed out started back up again.

A small group of villagers began to play on string, percussion, and wind instruments that held hints of familiarity but weren't immediately recognizable. One guy looked like he was playing a guitar, but it had too many strings and the shape wasn't quite the same.

As the folksy music picked up, men and women gathered around a large bonfire and began to dance.

The women wore red tunics with matching aprons and open skirts underneath with white embroidered skirts below that. Their red leather boots matched their tunics, and they each sported headbands made of flowers and flowing ribbons. They made quite the sight as they spun, and I would have appreciated the beauty of this cultural moment if I wasn't... you know, tied to a tree and possibly bleeding to death.

I mean, I'm all about the authentic local experience when traveling, but this was a little *too* authentic.

So head honcho dude noticed I was trying to weasel my way out of this seriously shitty situation and proceeded to slap the left side of my face with a thin wooden rod.

What the actual f—

Another whap!

I could feel the gashes in my face oozing fresh blood, the pain exploding in waves. I was going to kick that man's ass when I got out of this, I vowed.

But of course, I'm not Rambo, and I don't have any supernatural abilities that I know of, so all my outrage in the world didn't save me.

Obviously, since here I am.

The man who assaulted my face spoke rapidly in Ukrainian, but I'm more fluent in Russian, and even that's stretching things. Yana taught me the basics. I can say hello, goodbye, where's the bathroom, and make very basic conversation. I had a feeling I would need a hell of a lot more language skills than that to talk my way out of this, assuming I was ever allowed to speak again.

Oh gods, I could die without ever uttering another word.

What a strange thought.

What would my last words be if given the chance? I thought hard about this as the angry man screamed lustily at me, spittle flying from his lips, which sat in the middle of his face like a toad's mouth surrounded by hair.

But I did catch a few words.

And they left me paralyzed with fear.

Sacrifice.

God.

Death.

Don't ask me how I know these words in Ukrainian and not basic shit like how to order coffee. It involved a night of heavy drinking and watching *Game of Thrones* with Ukrainian subtitles.

At any rate, I was clearly doomed.

I was a George RR Martin character who had done the right thing and so obviously must pay with my life.

And now I'm waiting for a god to come and kill me.

Likely I'll just end up dying of hypothermia and blood loss by morning, and that will be the end of Evangeline Love.

I blink through blood again, which is mixing with my tears now.

The man seems satisfied I won't be making an escape anytime soon, so he turns his attention to a woman who joins him. She speaks harshly, her aged face lined with years and disapproval. He grunts, then proceeds to ignore her, much to her clear annoyance.

I feel ya there, sister.

But there can be no camaraderie right now. Since I'm still gagged and all.

Is she making an appeal for my release?

What is the point of all this?

I know Ukrainians aren't backwards people who use human sacrifice as a religious experience. From all Yana has told me, it's a beautiful country with kind people, despite its political turmoil.

There were no Yelp reviews that prepared me for this kind of treatment. I mean, I know Yana said to make sure I take my shoes off when entering someone's home, and to not show the bottom of my foot to someone when sitting before them, but One: I'm pretty sure I haven't had a chance to break any social niceties, and Two: this kind of punishment would be a tad overkill.

My wavering thoughts flicker to the poor souls who shared the plane with me. What happened to Yana? To the rest of the passengers and crew? Are they all dead? Did no one else survive? Or were they maybe found by a less sadistic village? That would be nice, if extremely optimistic.

My heart lurches at the memory of Yana's smile. Her laugh. Her unique way at looking at the world.

She can't be dead. It's not possible.

But of course it is.

We all die eventually. And none of us are guaranteed

another day with any certainty. I should know that more than most.

My thoughts are interrupted by a man standing to the side of the group holding an extremely long horn of some kind. He blows into it, and the music instantly stops, as does any dancing and chatter.

Everyone turns towards the forest, which is now darkening with long stretches of shadow cast by the rising full moon.

Something shifts in the energy of the villagers. The smell of fear catches on the wind, and people begin to fidget.

They clearly believe something big is about to happen.

Goosebumps form on my cold skin, despite my rational mind arguing that nothing scary is going to come out of that forest.

But does it really matter?

I'm going to die one way or another—that much is becoming clear.

At least dying by a mythical god-like creature in the Ukrainian woods would be more interesting than dying from the cold.

Is this how my parents and sister felt, I wonder? Did they know the end was coming, or was it as sudden and instant as the police said it was?

Is it better to know the moment of your impending death, or to be surprised by it?

Right now I'd rather be surprised.

Knowing isn't making this experience more fun.

As the final rays of sunlight disappear, the villagers follow suit, slipping into the shadows as torches are put out.

It only takes a moment before I am completely alone.

The blood in my eyes obscures my vision, and the pain

from my injuries is making me dizzy and nauseous. I rub my head back and forth against the tree, and finally manage to loosen the gag.

The world around me spins as my head lolls to the side, my neck no longer strong enough to support itself.

Snow begins to fall, thick and heavy, quickly coating the world around me with powdery white magic. It would be a sight to behold were I not dying.

I can't even feel the cold anymore. My body is going into shock, and I know I won't survive much longer. My head wound seeps blood. My face is raw and cut. Everything in me aches. The rope digs deeply into my skin, cutting flesh.

I'm nearly unconscious when I first see him stepping out of the shadows of the forest and into the moonlight. The god these villagers fear and worship in equal measure. He looks like a man from a distance. A tall, muscular man with a wild mess of short dark hair that accents his pale skin and clear blue eyes.

He wears a long black cape, black pants and a black shirt.

As he comes closer, I get a better view of him, and I startle at his face.

It's chiseled from stone, beautiful in its way, but covered in scars that mar that beauty with unspeakable pain.

His gaze latches on to mine, and once he is a few feet from me, he stops.

He speaks, saying something in Russian, though with a strange accent I don't recognize.

I try to speak, to explain that I speak limited Russian, but my words are mumbled. My mind is cloudy, and I can't find the words I need, so I switch to English. "I don't understand you. Please... help me. I'm... dying."

The taste of blood coats my tongue as I cough. Alarm

spreads through me, filling my veins with adrenaline. Panic wells within me, and I use the last of my strength to strain against the ropes.

The god-like man surprises me by speaking again, this time in broken English. "What crime you committed?" he asks, standing so still it's like he's become a part of the landscape.

"Crime?" I shake my head, a sob choking me. "My plane crashed. I didn't..." I cough again and more blood sprays from my mouth. "I didn't do anything wrong."

At least not here. Not now. Not this time.

I push away thoughts of my past. I don't want to die with my deepest regrets haunting me. I'd rather think about the happy moments in my life. Those are the memories I want to carry into the afterlife, whatever that may be for someone like me.

The man steps forward and leans down, bringing his mouth to my neck. He sniffs at me, as if testing a fine wine, then pulls back. I gasp when I see his mouth. His teeth are elongated unnaturally, and his eyes have turned black as night. "You innocent?"

Innocent? That's a hard word to unpack for me. The short answer is no. The long answer is yes I'm innocent of anything he might accuse me of, but there's so much more to me than this trip.

But I can't explain all that. I'm too far gone. I just shake my head.

As darkness engulfs me and I resign myself to my fate, I feel the ropes around me release and my body collapses into strong arms that lift me up and hold me close.

"You innocent," he whispers, and then he runs through the forest as I drift into darkness.

CHAPTER 2: WHERE THE HELL AM I AND HOW DID I GET HERE?

PAIN. Bone deep and splitting.

I try to scream but end up vomiting instead.

A large hand gently turns my head so I don't choke.

Gentle fingers—cool to the touch on my feverish face—brush back my hair.

Tears blur my eyes, but I open them wide enough to see I'm puking into a beautiful china bowl hand-painted in exquisite detail, and I feel a sudden surge of guilt for spoiling such a lovely piece of art.

When my guts are thoroughly spent, I fall back, and the hand supporting my head rests me against a pillow.

My eyes flicker, then I open them slowly, pushing past the pain.

It's his face I see in the candlelight. His dark eyes, penetrating and intelligent. His beautiful, scarred face locked in an unreadable expression. "Dying," he says, his mouth forming the English words with visible discomfort.

Tears trickle from my eyes, and I can't speak, so I nod.

"I save you," he says, and he holds out his arm, pulling up his sleeve. He is built of muscle, and I flinch as he takes a knife and cuts his wrist. A trail of blood pools to the surface of his skin and he holds it to my lips.

I recoil back, but I'm too weak to make much of a protest. Still, he doesn't force me to drink. He holds his arm out, waiting.

I take too long in my decision, and I watch in wonder as the cut he made stitches itself back together.

He's expressionless as he uses the knife to once again splay open his own flesh for me.

I nod, not wanting to see him cut himself open again.

He presses his wrist to my lips, and the blood leaks into my mouth.

I expect it to cause more nausea, to taste of iron and salt, but the moment it touches my tongue, a surge of power hits me, and I'm flush with it, with him.

Half delirious, the pain consuming every thought, I wrap my lips more tightly around his wrist and suck in the blood, drinking greedily. It's rich and viscous, savory and dark. Molasses and red wine with a hint of oak and moonbeams.

My pain recedes, and the panic surging through me dissipates as the dark shadow of death retreats.

I feel myself being called back to my body, to this world.

To him.

My vision clears, and I pull away, but his blood is still on my lips. Still pulsing with me. I feel a strange and sudden connection to this stranger before me. This feared god of the woods.

I feel an ache.

A need.

A fire newly lit.

I move towards him instinctively. He has one arm still around me, supporting me in the bed. I rub my face against that arm like a cat. I swear to the gods I almost purr.

What the hell is wrong with me?

I flinch back, away from the beckoning temptation of his muscled body, away from whatever this is that's pulling me towards him.

He glances away, his face unreadable.

But there's one part of his body he can't control, and it's at full attention, straining against the buttons of his pants.

Blood rushes to my face, but not from embarrassment— rather from mutual desire. I suddenly crave him more than I've ever craved anything or anyone.

He pulls away, settling me onto the bed as he steps back.

The separation is almost painful, and this time his face flinches, mirroring my own pain at the lack of contact between us.

I don't know this guy. This...

Okay, I'm going to say it, even though I sound like a complete lunatic right now...

But...

I've seen the same movies and read the same books as everyone else.

This man is a creature of the night, cold to the touch, and has teeth that suck blood...

The villagers called him a god.

But legends have a different name for him.

"Vampire," I say out loud. "You're a vampire, aren't you?"

He cocks his head, examining me quizzically, then speaks. But it's all in Russian.

I'm about to tell him I can't understand him, that's he's talking too fast and my language skills are limited, but something shifts inside me.

Something unexpected.

I can almost sense what he's trying to say.

A few words stand out. Words I didn't know before.

"Rest."

"Stay."

"Outside is dangerous."

My eyes widen, fear flooding my veins. But not fear of him, which is completely absurd. Or is it? Since I've been here, it's the humans who have tied me up, beat me, and left me for dead. He saved me, healed me, and gave me a safe place to sleep.

I learned a long time ago, don't believe what others think you should, believe what you know is right.

He might be a god, or a monster, or a vampire...but he's also my rescuer.

And then a thought occurs to me that I wish I could un-think.

The words slip out of my mouth before I have a chance to censor them. One of my many fatal flaws.

"Was I your dinner?" I ask in alarm.

He glances down, then walks away.

It's only now that there's distance between us that I have the attention to examine the rest of my surroundings. I'm in the strangest kind of room. It's large and made of stone, like the inside of a cave, but it's exquisite. The stone is carved into beautiful designs. Nature mostly, but also scenes of domestic life, of farming, of lovers under a cherry tree.

There's a fire in the center, a large pit with warm flames that dance across the walls and ceiling. It wasn't candlelight earlier, I realize, but firelight.

I'm in a four-poster bed that looks hand carved from a beautiful dark wood. I run my hand over the design, marveling at the detail.

The man is standing at the door, watching me take it all in.

"Did you do all this?" I ask. I don't know how I know, but I know.

He nods.

"It's... " I don't have words for it. "It's the most marvelous thing I've ever seen."

I don't know how well he understands me, but his face softens at my words, and a small smile begins to tug at the corner of his mouth.

"Sleep," he says in English, then walks through the door and closes it behind him.

As if his voice has the power to control my body, exhaustion overtakes me quite suddenly. I can no longer keep my eyes open, and I drift into a nightmare-less sleep for the first time in six years.

WHEN I WAKE, I feel more refreshed than I ever have in my life. My nightly terrors didn't haunt me for once, but the memory that inspires them still weighs heavy on my mind no matter how hard I try to push them away.

Little known fact: I was originally going to be a journalist. I wanted to travel the world chronicling the stories of others. But then...then everything changed. I changed. I saw the darkest parts of myself manifest and I knew my path had to change.

So I chose psychology, thinking maybe if I could understand the darkness of others, I could begin to understand my own.

Instead, I've just become more proficient at keeping

those memories locked in a mental box I prefer not to look in.

But this trip, this devastatingly fatal vacation, has once again reshaped me. Changed me.

However this ends, I won't be the same Evangeline who got on that plane in Los Angeles just a few days ago.

It's quite the marvel of humanity that one moment, one single second, can completely reshape who we are and the directions our lives follow. For better or worse. Often for worse.

My stomach rumbles, and my bladder aches, reminding me of my very human needs that no amount of trauma or crazy god-abductions can smother completely. I need to eat and pee, stat.

Also, my mouth feels like something died in it, but I'm not hopeful about finding a toothbrush anywhere around here. I wonder if my carry-on luggage was saved? Maybe someone in the village has it? It would have my cell phone, a change of clothes, toiletries. All things that would be incredibly useful right now.

Of course if I show up, will they just try to kill me again? Or will they be cool since their god favored me? I need a better guidebook than the one I bought for this trip, because I really don't know the rules.

I slide to the edge of the bed, testing my ability to stay upright. So far so good.

The fire is still burning strong, and the thick rug beneath me takes the sting out of the cold stone as I slowly stand and stretch my weary muscles.

I expect pain, aches, injuries, but I'm startled to discover my body works just fine. Better than fine. In fact, I have never in my life felt this strong, fast, limber, lithe...it's astonishing.

Memories of the night before come back to me like a dream. The abuse at the hands of the man in the village. The vampire who saved me and gave me his blood.

Holy shit, am I becoming a vampire?

I don't know how these things work. There are so many myths out there, and of course I assumed they were all bullshit.

But now? Now I know there's more to this world than I ever realized.

Vampires are *real*?

Before I can make a mad dash out of the room to find answers, I'm reminded once again of my need for a bathroom. And I also suddenly realize how badly I stink. I look down at my body and see that I'm still wearing the leggings and shirt I traveled in, only my clothes are torn and bloody and filthy.

I look around and see an arched doorway that leads to a hall. I follow it down a stone pathway into a large cavernous space with a waterfall pouring into a pool that's steaming with hot water. Beside it on a rock there's a pile of clean clothes. And in another corner there's what looks like a place to relieve my bladder... into a hole in the ground. I peer into the hole, but nothing putrid emanates from it. A crude toilet-like device is built over it, and I go on a leap of faith that I'm supposed to do my business here. If not, I'll definitely owe the vampire god an apology.

Once I'm done, I shed my clothing and step slowly into the hot pool. The water is almost too hot, but it soaks into my cold flesh invitingly, and I sink into it, enjoying the warmth it brings.

I'd love to spend the day lounging in this pool, enjoying the beauty of the flowers growing around me, the greenery that winds itself down the stone, despite this being the dead of winter. This is a magical place, and though I use that word euphemistically, I realize that might be literally true. After all, if vampires are real, maybe magic is too?

My pulse quickens at the thought.

As someone who grew up on books about schools for witches and doors to magical lands, I'm 100% down for finding some real magic in a world that is far too bleak most of the time.

Then my thoughts turn to Yana...my best friend. The one person who knew all my secret sins and still loved me. If she's dead, I need to find her body, get her to her family, and give her a proper resting place. If she's alive... Can she be alive?

This is all too much.

I wash my body quickly, my glance darting away from the scars that serve as a reminder of the monster I truly am.

Only my face was left undamaged.

My beautiful, perfect face.

My beauty is a lie I wear to cover up the monster that lives beneath.

But as I touch my face, I flinch, and tears burn my eyes.

I always thought that I would be happy if my face reflected the person I truly am.

There were even moments I was tempted to mar my own looks to end the lie.

But...

Now...

My stomach drops as I seek to find a still surface of the water where I can see my reflection.

When I do, I scream.

All the physical pain that the vampire took from me comes back ten fold when I see what I now look like.

Deep scars cut across my forehead and cheeks, one slashing across my eyebrow.

The blood healed the wounds but left the scars.

Some are from the crash. Some from the man with the wooden whip.

And now I have finally gotten my wish.

I look like the monster I always knew I was.

A sob racks my body, and I fall to my knees on the rocks and weep.

CHAPTER 3: DID I SOMEHOW FLY THROUGH A TIME PORTAL? WHAT THE HELL IS THIS NONSENSE, AND WHERE'S MY WIFI?

I DON'T KNOW how long I spend mired in self-pity, but I'm not one to stay in that state. My recovery time from trauma could be considered... cold. Heartless even. There are those who wallow in their pain. There are those who use their pain to become better people. There are those who ignore their pain entirely.

I tend to follow a progression. Wallow briefly, see what I can learn, then ignore.

I've already reached the ignore stage when I pull myself up from the stone ground and make my way to the pile of clothes my unusual host left for me.

There will be time later to figure out the impact these new, more visible scars, will have on my life and self-esteem. Right now I'm just grateful to be alive, and I need to figure out how to get out of this village and get to Kyiv, where the US Embassy can hopefully help me get home. Since I don't know that I'll be able to recover my passport or personal items at this point.

I dress quickly in clothes that are far too large. They clearly belong to the vampire, which makes sense. He at least included a sash to tie the pants so they don't fall off as I walk.

Still, the effect is comical as I make my way back to my room and out the main door into a long stone hall carved with more scenes and lit by torches that look...odd. Off somehow. I hold my hand near one, and though it emanates warmth, it's not a real flame, but some kind of blue ball of light. I take one off the wall and carry it with me, the extra illumination giving me a false sense of safety.

It's time to explore.

The hall has doors leading to different rooms, but they're all locked and require the kind of large, ancient key my mother liked to collect before she died.

Moving on, following the red carpet beneath me, I arrive at a banquet hall with a large stone table, another fire pit burning brightly, and a room off to the side. I'm hoping it's a kitchen, and it is, but there's nothing edible that I can see. Instead, it has a pot boiling over a fire that smells bitter, and herbs hanging everywhere, with bottles of strange things lining shelf after shelf. It looks more like a medieval scientist's workshop than the kitchen it once was, and I don't think any food has been made in here in a very long time.

I shiver when I recall that I was likely supposed to be my host's dinner last night.

Which begs the question, if not me, then who? If he can't eat food, he needs someone's blood, right?

Why didn't he eat me, I wonder?

He thought I was guilty of something.

Does he only eat the guilty?

I frown. If that's true, then I deserve to be his next meal.

My search continues for food, but when I come across a jar of eyeballs, I give up, my appetite no longer what it was.

What does he do in here? Who is this creature?

I keep exploring and next find a library stacked with books and ancient scrolls. My jaw drops open as I study the titles. They are mostly in Russian, though some are in a language I don't recognize. I do find a small section of English books, though they were written before there was any agreement on consistent spelling, so they're almost as hard to read as the Russian.

There's a desk in the corner that looks well used, and I berate myself for being surprised that the man who saved me would be well read. I had him pegged as a sort of barbarian monster, but none of us are what we seem, are we?

Anyone meeting me before my trip here would have thought me a kind, lovely person—albeit with a dark sense of humor.

Maybe now people will see me and know me for what I truly am.

I shove a book back into its spot and leave, still searching for a way out.

It's foolish to go back to the village, but I need answers, and I need to get out of here. Maybe I can steal a horse or something and ride until I find a sane town that won't try to feed me to its resident monster.

By complete accident, I stumble upon the sleeping form of my rescuer in what looks like a guest room. Similar to the room I woke up in, but simpler and smaller. He must have given me his room and slept in here.

The thoughtfulness sends a ping of guilt through me, knowing I'll be leaving and not coming back.

His body is so still he looks dead, and there's no movement in his chest.

I step closer, feeling the same pull from last night wash over me.

The desire.

The lust.

The need.

The connection.

What is this? Is it a spell? Magic? An effect from his blood?

I can't help myself as I put a hand over his chest, my body buzzing with the taboo of it all. The danger. The exhilaration and excitement.

Will he wake?

Will he bite me?

Will I make it out of here alive?

When my palm touches his chest, it is still. Nothing moves. No heartbeat. No breath. Nothing.

As I'm about to pull away, though, something happens.

A beat.

Just one.

But it's something.

Then another.

And then the man with the scarred face sucks in a breath, his eyes still closed, his body still inert, and his heart rate increases until it's a steady pulse under my palm.

My eyes widen, and I feel his blood inside me still, responding to his heart, pulsing with the beat, as if we are tied to each other.

I snatch my hand away and move quickly to the door, terror and arousal warring within me. My mind is clouded, my body covered in a sheen of sweat.

Before he can wake, I dash out of the room, closing the door softly behind me, and then lean my back against it as I try to catch my breath.

What just happened?

His heart was silent, and then it wasn't.

Is that normal?

What the hell do I know about normal for Russian vampires anyways?

I run through the halls, more frantic this time, needing to find a way outside. Needing fresh air, even if it's freezing.

He didn't leave me a coat, likely assuming I would stay inside, so I find a fur blanket and throw it over my shoulders once I discover the way out.

The cave opening, which is blocked by a large oak door.

It takes all my strength to push the beast of a door open, and I know intuitively that I would not have been able to do this a few days ago. The blood within me is making me stronger.

Let's hope that happy side effect lasts.

Outside it is a bright cold day. Snow covers the ground, but the sky is clear and the sun is shining. I inhale the fresh air and tilt my face to the heavens with a small smile before I begin my trek into the village.

Assuming I can find my way.

But I have a secret super power, as my family used to call it.

I'm ridiculously good with directions. I can find my way anywhere. Even places I've never been. It's an instinct I've learned to listen to over the years and makes me a great travel companion for my friends.

Trusting my intuition, I head north and see the tracks made last night by the vampire carrying me to his den. Bingo!

I slow my pace as the village comes into view, hut-like homes made of stone and wood lining the dirt-packed streets. I'm standing on a hill, which gives me a good view of the surrounding area. There are farms further back, and one building that looks like a church in the center of the village surrounded by the marketplace. It's bustling today, likely due to the nice weather, as families trade with each other.

I need to find help, someone sympathetic. My mind turns to last night, to the woman who stood up to the man with the whip. Maybe she'd be willing to help me, if I can find her.

Keeping trees in my path, I slink closer to the village, fear making the blood in my body pump harder.

I definitely do not want to run into that sadistic man again. But if I do, at least I won't be unconscious and injured this time.

It doesn't take me long to reach the edge of the village, and as I'm about to leave the forest I hear something. A sound in the bushes. Probably just a wild animal.

Though I realize with alarm that the woods are unnaturally quiet.

No birds.

No animals scurrying up the trees.

Nothing.

That's not normal.

I freeze, staying very still, and move towards the direction of the sound.

Cuz I'm smart like that.

I'd definitely be the first one to die in a horror movie. That's a given.

Something whips past me, knocking me into a bush. I fall to my hands and knees, blinking in confusion at what I've landed on.

And then I scream.

I can't help it.

Because I'm knee deep in the remains of something that used to be human.

Now it's a pile of shredded meat and blood and bone. A

sharp edge cuts my hand as blood seeps into my clothes and stains my skin.

Acid coats my throat.

The smell gags me, and I scramble back, my mind shutting down as instinct and survival takes over.

I can't get away. The entrails follow me, stuck to my clothes.

And then other shouts. Commands in harsh, staccato Russian.

Three women emerge from the shadows of the forest carrying swords or spears, and all the pointy bits are aimed at me.

I hold my hands up, a bit of intestine dangling from my ring finger.

"*Pomogite!*" I say. "Help!"

They make gestures and say things I don't understand. "*Pozhaluysta!*" My tongue feels swollen and my skin is crawling. "*Pozhaluysta, pomogite.*" Help, please. I'm begging, but they are not persuaded. I try to explain in broken Russian that I don't understand. That I didn't do this. One of the women pokes me with a spear and forces me to stand and begin walking into the village, but we are stopped by the woman I've been looking for. The woman who seemed to speak up for me last night.

She studies me with shrewd eyes. "You are still alive. How surprising."

"You speak English?" I say with visible relief.

"I do. How is it you survived a night with our god? No others have."

So my suspicions were correct. I was meant to be dinner. Why did he spare me? "I honestly have no idea. He healed me. Now I'm just trying to find a way out of here. I need to get to the US Embassy. Can you help me?"

She looks to the women holding their weapons at me, and at her sharp command, they drop them. "Come with me but be quick. Others will not be so kind."

I scramble to follow her as she leads me behind the village and into her house through a back door. Once inside, her guards disappear into other rooms, and the woman hands me a rough towel and a basin of water. "Clean yourself. I will bring you clothes."

Her home is simple, with tapestries hanging on the wall, a fireplace with a pot over it, a kitchen and living room all in one space, and a bedroom upstairs. I do my best to clean up, then at her insistence I undress and put on the skirt and blouse she hands me.

"I am Varvara," she says. "But friends call me Vara."

"I'm Evangeline." I don't know that I have friends here, so I leave it at that.

She offers me a seat in front of the fire, and I take it and accept a cup of tea and a plate of biscuits from her. "Thank you," I say. "I'm starving."

I'm amazed I have an appetite after what I've seen, but I eat anyways, knowing I need strength. When I've finished, which only takes a few minutes, I turn to her. "Who killed that person?" I ask.

She frowns. "Our village is cursed," she says. "A creature of the night hunts us at night, killing our friends and family."

I freeze with my tea cup halfway to my lips. "The god? The creature you gave me to? Is he doing this?"

She nods. "We have appeased him for centuries with the blood of the guilty, to satiate his hunger, but it is not enough. Now he attacks during the day. We do not know why or how this has changed, but it will be the end of us if he is not stopped."

"So... my plane crashes, and instead of helping me, you tie me up and offer me as sacrifice to the creature killing you? What the hell is wrong with you people?" I ask, forgetting any manners.

She sighs deeply. "It is not what I would have done, were I in charge. But I am not. We are at the whims of a power-hungry dictator who rules our village with cruelty and bloodlust."

My head is spinning from all this. "What about the others in the plane? My friend? Were there any other survivors?"

She shakes her head. "You are the only one we found. We didn't even find the plane. Just you."

"But that doesn't make sense. There has to be wreckage. Bodies or survivors. Something?"

She stands and walks to a corner, then returns with a familiar backpack. "We found this by your body."

I reach for it, tears stinging my eyes at the one piece of home I have left. My canvas bag with patches sewn into it from my world travels. I spent most of my 20s searching the world for the missing piece inside myself, never finding anything other than more missing pieces.

I clutch it to my chest with a sob. "Thank you."

She studies me, and a nervous energy moves through me.

She opens a trunk and pulls out a large wooden stake. "You may be our only hope. You are the only person ever to get so close to the creature. Kill him. Stab him through the heart with this stake while he sleeps. Free our village of this curse."

She hands it to me, and I feel the death it carries as I clutch it.

We are both startled from our conversation by a banging at the door. An angry Russian voice demanding entry.

Vara rises and grabs my arm. "Quickly. Leave. That is Boris, the one who tied you up. You do not want him finding you," she whispers, guiding me to the back door. "Run! And remember what I said! Kill the creature before he kills us all."

I shove the stake into my backpack, throw it over my shoulders and run with everything in me. Away from the village. Away from the cave where the monster lives. Away from it all and towards what I hope is civilization.

When I reach the edges of the woods, I step out into an open field covered in snow, but the moment I do I find myself at the beginning of the forest again.

I blink. Confused. And I run again, to the edge of the woods, to the open field.

I step out, and once again I'm returned to my starting point.

My heart beats against my chest erratically. I pant, not from exertion but from confusion and fear.

I unzip my bag and pull out my phone, trying frantically to get a signal, but there's nothing. Not even a sliver of a bar.

I try again, running to different locations, but it all results in the same thing.

Anytime I try to leave, I end up at the beginning.

Realization dawns on me, and I sink to my knees in defeat.

Vara didn't tell the whole truth.

This village is cursed.

But not just with a monster hunting them.

I cannot leave this village.

It won't let me.

CHAPTER 4: THE PART WHERE I DECIDE WHETHER TO STAB THIS WOODEN STAKE INTO SOMEONE'S HEART. NEVER THOUGHT THAT WOULD BE ONE OF MY LIFE CHOICES.

FOR THE FIRST time in my life, I'm lost.

Truly and legitimately lost.

And I don't know what to do about it.

I've been wandering the forest for hours, and as the sun sets, the chill in the air grows, mirroring the bone deep frost forming in my bones.

How many times can I flirt with death before he comes to claim me for good?

Everywhere I turn, everything looks the same.

The same trees, the same rocks, the same bushes, the same snow. I don't know if it's the curse trapping me in this spot, or if I've lost my wits, but I can't find the village, or the cave or anything else for that matter.

The fear doesn't truly steal my resolve until the night descends, covering the world in darkness. Even the moon, still looking full in the sky, seems to have a hard time penetrating the deep purple shadows settling around me.

And then the storm comes. Rain and sleet pour from the sky like bullets meant to kill or maim their target. This isn't a docile Christmas scene one might envision Santa Claus in. This is more like what Santa's evil twin would travel in.

Winter has come, indeed.

I chuckle at the reference despite myself.

Let's just hope George RR Martin isn't writing my story, or I'm unlikely to live through it.

Huddling under the largest tree I can find, pulling the cloak Vara gave me tightly around my shoulders, I close my eyes and pray to gods I don't believe in that I'll make it through the night.

When I hear the inhumane sound of a fierce beast, I know my prayers have not been heard.

I don't see the creature.

But I hear him.

Lurking.

Hunting.

Stalking.

I try to stay still. To calm my breathing. To hold my fear deep within lest it betray me.

Why would the man who saved me the night before want to kill me tonight?

Because I escaped? Because I disobeyed his orders to stay inside?

He warned me, and I didn't listen.

Story of my life.

I never see him. He is only ever the air around me, whooshing past. The breath on my neck. The nightmare of my dreams.

Except nothing he can do can compete with my actual nightmares. That's the part he doesn't understand. How can I fear the monster he is, when I already live with a much worse monster every day of my life?

So I stand and I cry out into the night. I scream and I cry and I challenge the beast to come and get me.

"You want to kill me?" I scream. "Then do it. Do it! I'm ready. I've been ready for six long years. End my life right now, you piece of shit. You'd be doing me a favor."

The wind steals my voice and carries it far and wide, and I feel a lightening of my soul at finally saying what I've been too afraid to acknowledge before.

It should have been me who died.

And now it will be.

I'm already resigned to my death when I feel him close by, his presence no longer the weirdly familiar feeling I had in the cave. Now he feels all monster, and I'm ready for him.

He comes from behind, and I don't turn around.

Something sharp slashes across my back.

I fall to the ground, already close to unconsciousness when he pulls me to my feet and digs his fangs into the flesh of my neck.

Searing pain floods me.

I strain to see his face, to look into his eyes and force him to watch me die.

But that moment never comes.

Instead, I see only darkness.

I WAKE in the cave again, in the same bed, with the same fire, in a case of total déjà vu. Well, shit.

How am I still alive?

The fresh taste of *his* blood answers that question. He healed me again. But why attack me just to heal me?

What the hell is happening here? I'm starting to feel like I'm on a massively bad drug trip and am hallucinating this whole thing, but that's highly unlikely given I've never done drugs.

But our minds are powerful things and will do anything to help us make sense of things, including lie to us if necessary.

"I told you no leaving," a voice says from the shadows, startling me from my thoughts.

"You!" I try to sit up, but a wave of dizziness forces me back onto the pillows. "Why didn't you just finish me off?" I ask.

He comes into the light, and I realize he's injured. His face has a new gash on it that oozes blood, but it doesn't seem to be healing.

And he's limping.

"What...what happened to you? Why am I here?" He doesn't understand my words, and I pound the bed in frustration. I should have studied Russian with more gusto.

I can feel frustration coming from him in waves, and he holds out his hand, beckoning me to take it.

Oh, why the hell not? In for a penny, in for a pound, as they say.

I take his hand, and he helps me gingerly off the bed. My body aches, but it's nothing compared to last night. He limps forward and nearly stumbles into the wall. I catch his body, and holy shit he weighs a ton. I nearly topple over from his weight.

Still, he rights himself and keeps walking, and I follow him to a door that he opens with an ancient skeleton key.

My breath hitches when I see what is within.

Paintings everywhere. Covering the walls, stacked in piles, with a fresh one on an easel half finished.

And they're all of the same thing.

A hideous monster of darkness and shadow, fangs long

and dripping with blood, body deformed and scarred. I look to him and to the paintings pointing. "Is this how you see yourself? Is this you?" I ask.

He shakes his head and rummages through his paintings, pulling one out that has two figures on it. He speaks rapidly in Russian, but like the last time, I start to inexplicably understand some of what he says, and I feel that same thrumming inside me as before.

"This me. This monster," he says, pointing to the figures.

Now I see it, and suddenly everything clicks into place.

My eyes fill with tears as the painting seems to come to life before my very eyes. The vampire in the painting is an exact likeness of the man before me, without modesty or embellishment. And he's fighting the creature of darkness, who has human entrails hanging from his mouth. The scene unfolds. The creature is eating the human, the vampire fights the creature. The creature dies, leaving the vampire badly wounded. On the painting, night turns to day turns to night, and the creature rises from the dead and kills again. The cycle repeats.

I have no idea what kind of magic this is, but I finally understand what's going on.

"You're fighting the creature?" I ask, turning to him. "The creature is killing people in the village and you're...you're protecting them?"

He nods.

"You're injured," I say, stating the obvious.

Fear grips me.

"You need to heal."

He looks away from me, but I feel his need for blood.

I look back at the painting, more pieces clicking. "When that monster injures you, it doesn't heal like normal, does it?"

"No," he says.

"You need blood to heal," I say.

He nods.

I sigh.

Shit is complicated in this little village.

I glance once more at his collection of grotesque art, then take his hand and drag him back to the bedroom. I find my backpack by the side of the bed and pull out the stake. He narrows his eyes at me but doesn't move. I make him sit on the bed, and I sit next to him.

"The village thinks you are killing people. They wanted me to kill you. Do you understand?"

He shakes his head and frowns.

I toss the stake into the fire pit. "We need to make them see the truth," I say. "But first, you have to heal."

I tilt my head, exposing my neck. "Can you feed from me without killing me?" I ask.

He shakes his head and moves away from me.

Ugh. Men. "You were totally the type who refused to go to the doctor when you were sick, weren't you?" I ask, but he doesn't understand. I might as well be talking to myself.

I'm about to berate him some more, but he groans, and I see blood seeping through his shirt. I step over to him and lift the fabric to check the wound. It's deep. Gouging. Fatal.

He doubles over, crashing onto the mattress with a deep moan, his eyes fluttering closed.

Shit.

I don't even know his name, I realize, as I try to revive him. "Hey there. Wake up. Come on, you can't die on me."

The glint of a knife on the table by the bed catches my eye, and I know what I must do.

Without pausing to think too long, I take the blade and slice it up my arm. The sting comes a moment later, followed by a deep and painful ache. I hold my arm over his lips, forcing the blood into his mouth. It doesn't take long for him to latch on and begin sucking.

The pain recedes almost instantly, turning to the most intense pleasure I've ever felt.

My arousal is instant and all consuming, but there's little I can do about it.

I'm entirely too lightheaded by the time his hunger is satiated, and I fall onto the bed beside him, exhausted, as we both sleep off our attacks.

Hours later, I'm woken by a gentle hand on my arm. "What have you done?" he asks.

In perfect English.

I open my eyes in surprise and find myself staring into his. "You speak my language now?"

He frowns and shakes his head. "No. I do not. It's much more complicated than that."

I sit up in the bed. Our bodies are touching, our emotions wrapped around each other's. "Explain then."

He caresses my face with his hand, and it sends a shiver up my spine. "What is your name?"

"Evangeline Love," I say. "But my friends call me Angel. Or Love."

"Angel... " he tests the name on his tongue like a new flavor. "I am Ivan."

"It's...nice to meet you, Ivan. I'm glad we can communicate now. But, are you going to tell me what's going on?"

He takes my hand and presses it to his chest. I feel his heart thump, just as I did the other night.

"The villagers left you for me to drink from. As a sacrifice," he says.

"Yeah, I got that part. So why didn't you partake?"

"When I came close to you, something happened." He

frowns, looking down at my hand still on his chest. "My heart hasn't beat for hundreds of years. But when I met you, it beat again for the first time." His eyes are luminous as he stares into my soul. "I thought it was a myth. A fairytale for monsters."

"What was?"

"The tales of the one true mate," he says in answer. "There were stories that if a vampire finds their one true mate, their heart will beat again, and if their mate is a vampire, they will be able to feed off each other alone for all of eternity."

My heart skips a beat at this. "So...you're saying I'm your mate?"

He nods. "And you completed the ritual. I would have warned you. That's why I didn't want to drink from you. You didn't know what that would mean, but I did. By sharing blood, we have bonded for eternity. Where you go, I go. If you die, I die. And vice versa. We are forever connected."

"Oh shit. So if I stabbed you with that stake, I'd be taking my own life too?"

He nods.

"And if that monster kills you, he kills both of us?"

He nods again.

"And this can't be undone?" I ask, but in my heart, I don't want it undone. I know literally nothing about this dude, so it's stupid as hell, but everything in me wants to be with him forever. Except...

I jump from the bed and away from him, though it pains me to do so. "This is a mistake. You don't want me. I'm the completely wrong person," I say as sobs rack my body against my will.

He reaches for me, but I push him away.

"Why do you say these things?" he asks.

Through the tears, I look up at him. "Look at me. Look at my face. At my scars. I'm not beautiful. Not anymore. I'm a monster."

He narrows his eyes at me as if to say, and? Have you seen my face lately?

I hiccup, thrown off track by this weird telepathy we have.

"That's not all though," I say. "The night you found me, you asked me if I was guilty. I didn't get a chance to tell you everything. I didn't get a chance to tell you the truth."

He raises an eyebrow at me. "Then tell me now. Why shouldn't I love you and take you as my mate, Evangeline Love?"

"Because I'm the real monster," I say. And then I tell him my dark secret. The thing even my best friend in the world doesn't know. "The worst kind of monster there is." I suck in a breath, steeling myself for what I'm about to say. "You should have fed on me that night. I deserve to die."

"Why?" he asks, his voice calm, his large, muscular body a rock for me to lean against. But I can't. Not now. Not until he knows the truth.

"Because six years ago, I killed my whole family."

CHAPTER 5: WHERE WE DRINK TOO MUCH HOMEMADE VODKA AND TELL ALL OUR SECRETS.

I SHIVER AND HICCUP, which is a really weird reaction to telling someone the truth, but there it is. I get hiccups when I confess grave sins.

Ivan places his large hand on mine, thin scars—almost like veins—running over his pale skin. "You do not have to speak of this if you do not wish to," he says in a deep, sexy voice.

At this point, if I'm being totally honest with myself, everything he says and does is sexy. Maybe that's the way it's supposed to go with the mate bond thing, I don't know, but it's distracting as hell. It's really hard to get your emo angst going on when you're turned on, ya know?

I hiccup again as a reply, and he raises an eyebrow and leaves me for a moment to open the drawer by the bed. He pulls out two crystal glasses and a bottle of clear liquid, then pours each of us a generous cup.

"Drink," he says, handing it to me. "It will warm your body and loosen your tongue, if that is what you wish."

That sounds ominous.

So naturally I do as he says. We clink glasses and I drink deeply and nearly spit it all out. "This is vodka," I say.

He nods, not even flinching as he drinks. Is this a Russian thing or a vampire-god thing?

"You know I've hardly eaten in days. If I drink this, I'll be sick."

He frowns. "It has been so long since my own humanity that I have forgotten how many needs you have to keep you alive." He sets his cup down. "Give me a moment. I will return and then we will talk, and you will try to convince me of your monstrous nature, and I will show you how wrong you are."

His words send shivers down my spine. If only I could latch onto them and believe that they were true.

I gingerly sip at the vodka while I wait for him to return, and I consider what my life is going to look like moving forward. I'm bonded to a vampire? This means I'll likely have to become a vampire, right? This is so freaking weird.

Which is, like, the understatement of the year. And also feels perverse. Why should I be the one to live forever after all I've done?

Ivan returns with a platter of food so tantalizing my eyes nearly pop out of my head. "Where did you get that?" I ask. "Certainly not from that place you call a kitchen." I shudder at the memory of the eyeballs in a glass jar.

He grins. "I have my ways, which I will elaborate on once you finish telling me your secrets." He places the tray on a table in front of the fireplace, and I join him as we each take a chair.

I fill my belly in silence, while he waits patiently, watching me with unreadable eyes. His mere presence calms something inside me that hasn't felt settled in six long, hellish years.

He makes me feel safe. Loved. Accepted.

Let's see if that's still true after what I tell him.

I finish my meal—a delicious mix of vegetables, meats, berries, and some kind of tart—and down the rest of my vodka. He smirks and refills both of our glasses.

The heat of the liquor burns through my veins, and I feel myself falling into that strange place we go when too much alcohol is consumed.

Ivan was right. This is loosening my tongue.

I reach over and pat his head. "You aren't going to like me very much after this," I tell him confidently, and my sadness creeps through our bond.

But he just shakes his head. "You tell me your story, and I'll tell you mine. We'll see who likes whom when this night is done."

"Fair enough," I say. Though I'm pretty sure I will definitely come out in the naughty corner compared to the hero before me who risks his life nightly to protect a village who blames him for the deaths.

Anyways.

Here goes.

"Six years ago, my parents and little sister helped me pack up our car and trailer so we could all drive from Utah, where we lived, to Los Angeles, where I was meant to start college. I was the first person in my family to go to college, so it was a big deal, and everyone was really proud and excited. My mom and dad were going to share the driving, but I argued with them. I was an adult and I wanted to be the one to drive myself to college. I'd had my license for a year, and I felt confident I could make the trip, no problem. They didn't want me to do it. They thought I wasn't ready, but I insisted. I went so far as to tell them I would go by myself if they didn't let me. I was a complete brat." I pause, emotion choking my throat, and I take another swig of vodka.

Ivan listens patiently, with a stillness that no human could master.

I suck in a breath and continue. "Long story short, they gave into my temper tantrum and let me drive. My mom had it all mapped out. She's detail oriented that way. But I've always had an instinct for directions, and I knew there was a shorter way. So while they were sleeping, I took a shortcut, knowing it would trim a few hours off our trip. I was excited to surprise them when they woke up."

A sob breaks in my throat, and tears burn my eyes, but I grit my jaw, take another shot, and keep talking. "They were surprised all right," I say with a sardonic laugh. "It started to rain. A true storm. And my shortcut had a hairpin turn I wasn't expecting. I took it too fast, the roads were too slick, and our car ran off the cliff."

Breathe. Just breathe. In and out. Ivan places a hand on mine, the weight of it a reassurance I don't deserve, but I selfishly take in anyways. "It's all a blur. The screaming. The crying. My little sister shrieking. And then the silence. When I woke, the car was totaled, and they were all dead. I was the only one left alive. It took hours for rescuers to find us. I couldn't move. I was too badly injured. I could only lie there with my dead family, staring into their open eyes."

Finally I look up and into Ivan's eyes. I need to see the moment he turns away from me. The moment he recognizes what kind of woman he bonded to. "I killed them. My self-ishness and stubbornness and recklessness killed them. I'm a monster."

Ivan moves closer to me, spreading his legs so that mine are between his. He reaches for my face, caressing the scars on my cheek with a gentle finger. "You are not a monster,

Love," he says. "You are still an Angel. My Angel. You made a mistake, as we all do. But you didn't kill your family, an accident did. It wasn't your fault. And they wouldn't want you to spend your life blaming yourself for this. They would undoubtedly want you to live a happy and fulfilled life, would they not?"

Tears flow now, and all the pain I've been holding unleashes like a flood from me. Ivan pulls me into his arms and holds me close, his strong, muscular body providing strength and safety as I release the pain that's been festering in me since the accident. "You don't think I'm a monster?" I ask.

"No, Love. I know you are not. I have met monsters before. I know what they look like. You are not one."

I pull back when I feel his emotions crash through me. Pain, sorrow, guilt. All mirrors of my own.

"Tell me," I whisper. "Tell me your story, Ivan."

He looks up at my use of his name, and I feel another wave of emotion, this time of love, of gratitude. He's been alone so long. Protecting a village that shuns him. Cut off from humanity, from his own humanity even. A monster in a cave, but that's not who he is.

"To tell you my story, I must tell you another story. The story of the Alchemist and the Apprentice," he says, then fills his glass with more vodka and begins his tale.

LONG AGO THERE lived an orphaned boy whose parents had died of the plague. He had no siblings, nor any other relatives, and when the village elder asked if anyone wished to take the boy in, no one did. Perhaps because the boy was small and pale and weak. Perhaps because everyone already had enough mouths to feed. Perhaps because the plague had decimated their small village, and there were none left to care for the fate of one such as him.

The boy's home, little more than a shack, was confiscated by the village council, and the boy was given the choice to live in the streets or be banished to the woods. Even at such a tender age, he knew he wouldn't last long in the woods, so he chose the streets.

He made a home on the rooftop of the old church with a bed of dirty straw someone left outside their barn. It stank and grew mildew, but it was the best he could manage. At night, he slept under the stars, giving each of them names, and praying it didn't rain. By day, he went down to the marketplace in his ragged clothing and asked those who passed by for food, but they had none to give. He went hungry for a day. Then two. On the third day, he tried to swipe an apple from a trader's cart, but he was caught, and would have lost his good hand if he hadn't quickly run into the woods where only hunters and soldiers dared to go.

His mother had told him stories about the forest. Stories of wolves and stories of witches that live in moving houses. The boy saw none of these things, but he did find a cherry tree and proceeded to fill his belly. He ate faster and longer than he ever had before. He ate even when it began to rain. When the boy was finished, he turned around and realized he could not remember which way it was back to the village. He tried to look for his footsteps, but the water had washed them all away.

The boy wandered for half a day. He had still not found his way back when the sun began to set. He had found no more food, save for a red mushroom sprinkled with white dots, and his mother warned him not to eat those.

When it became too dark to make his way through the

forest—and with a moonless night providing no light—the boy found the softest spot he could and lay down to sleep. He knew he was in danger, staying alone in the woods at night, but he had no other choice.

He woke in the early morning, before the sun had begun to rise, to the sound of a strange and scary beast growling in the shadows. The boy hardly had time to react when a man's shape came forward, slaying the beast with a long spear as easily as the boy might squash a bug.

The boy became instantly enamored with the man, and insisted on following him home, back to the elaborate caves that were spoken of only in hushed whispers in town.

The boy felt sure he would finally see a witch, or magic, or something equally amazing. What he found was something far more significant, though much more work than he expected.

For the man was an alchemist, and he agreed to take the boy on as an apprentice. The boy worked hard. He cleaned, cooked, mended, dried herbs, memorized ingredients and recipes, and studied hard. He had never been taught to read, but he learned fast, and over the years he became an accomplished alchemist in his own right.

The man viewed the boy as his son and took pride in the boy's talents and accomplishments. But one day, the boy came home excited about a new scroll he'd acquired that promised immortality. The man knew of such tales but was wise enough to never dabble in such dark magic. Those spells were for evil casters and witches, not alchemists. But the boy persisted, and after many years, finally brewed the potion that would make him immortal.

The man and the boy had their first true argument, and the man banished the boy from his home if he persisted in such evil enterprises.

The boy left, vowing to complete what he started.

It was a fortnight before the man saw the boy again, but he was no longer a boy. He now had the form of pure evil. His skeletal, monstrous body protruded with oozing sores and he stank of death and evil.

"Master, I have returned, more powerful than you can imagine," the creature said.

"Be gone with you," the Master replied in disgust. "You have tainted our craft with your needless ambitions. You do not deserve to call yourself an alchemist!"

The creature roared and screamed, filling the lands with an agonizing cry that would resonate in the nightmares of the people for many lives. "I will show you just how powerful I am!"

That night, under the glow of the full moon, the monster used his power for one last potion, and with it cast a dark curse on his home village. None shall leave who enter, and those who stay shall sate his hunger.

From that night forward, the creature terrorized the village, killing at will.

"Why do you do this?" the Master asked.

"They did the same to me, did they not? They cast me out when I was a child, cold and hungry and grieving the death of my family. They deserve to pay."

And so the Master did the only thing he could. He killed his apprentice, and that night he sobbed for hours at the evil he had done.

But the next night, the monster returned, gloating in his power. "I have proven to you I am the greatest alchemist the world has ever seen," the creature said. "I cannot be killed."

And so the master and the monster battle nightly. Every night the monster dies, and every night he is reborn.

He is called the Koschei, and it is said he cannot be

killed until his soul is found. But his soul is hidden separate from his body. It was cast into a needle, which is in an egg, which is in a duck, which is in a hare, which is in a crystal chest, which is buried under a green oak tree. As long as his soul is safe, he cannot die. If the chest is dug up and opened, the hare will bolt away. If it is killed, the duck will emerge and try to fly off.

There is only one true way to kill Koschei. If anyone possesses the egg that contains the needle that contains his soul, they can control the monster. And if the egg or needle is broken, Koschei will die his final death. So it is written.

WE SIT STILL for many long minutes while I process the story he's told me. My hand grips him more tightly, and I hold his gaze. "You're the alchemist in the story," I say. And it all makes sense. The jars, the potions, the strange magic of this place. And the monster... "And each night you have to fight the monster who was once like a son to you and watch him kill others."

Ivan nods. "So you tell me, Love. Which of us is the greater monster? I unleashed true evil into this world, one who is killing innocents. And now he kills during the day, during the time I cannot protect the people. I have failed."

CHAPTER 6: WHAT IS LOVE? BABY DON'T HURT ME, DON'T HURT ME, NO MORE. HEY, DON'T JUDGE. IT'S A LEGIT SONG AND FITS WHAT'S ABOUT TO HAPPEN, OKAY? JUST KEEP READING.

HIS PAIN ENTERS ME, a mirror of my own. This bond we have connects us in ways more intimate than anything I've ever experienced. It draws me to him. Not just because of the magic, but because of what I can feel within him. What he can feel within me.

We are one.

We share all.

I reach for him. My heart is full. I want to erase his pain. Show him how beautiful he is to me. To the world.

"You are the hero of the story, not the villain," I tell him. "You cannot control the deeds of others."

I place my palm against his cheek, and he closes his eyes, a feeling of peace washing over us both. "You've done everything you can for this village. They need to know the truth."

His eyes open, his gaze holding mine. "They know the truth," he says, shocking me.

My hand drops, and I stare, mouth agape. "What do you mean?"

"The village elder, he knows. He knows I defend the village night after night. We have spoken."

"What? You've spoken to Boris? That jackass who scarred my face?"

Ivan's eyes narrow. "He did this to you?"

I nod. "I was injured in the plane crash, but yes, he whipped my face with a wooden rod, leaving the wounds that you healed that night."

Ivan's teeth elongate, and I feel the rage bubbling in him, but it doesn't scare me. I know that anger could never be directed at me. We are bonded. We protect each other.

"I will kill him," he says.

The vodka is wearing off remarkably fast, maybe because of the vampire blood in me, and my mind is gaining clarity. "We need a plan. You said in your story that Koschei can be controlled if someone finds the egg his soul is in?"

Ivan nods.

"And he's suddenly attacking during the day? He's never done that before?"

"He hasn't, this is true."

The wheels in my mind turn. "What if Boris found the egg? And he's trying to pit the village against you, so he can kill you off and let Koschei run free?"

"Why would he do such a thing?" Ivan asks.

"Men in power will do anything to keep that power," I say. "And he's getting some challenge from Vara. Maybe he wants to keep the women in their place. It wouldn't be the first time."

"I must turn you," Ivan says. "We must make you immortal. You will be safer. Harder to kill. And we will gain strength from each other and be able to feed on each other for power."

I hesitate. "I...this is hard. After what I've done to my

family, why should I be the one to live forever? And...if I do...I'll never see them again." My voice grows thick with tears. "I don't know what the afterlife holds, but I had hoped...I had hoped I would one day be with them again, so I could apologize. So they could know how sorry I am and how much I regret my choices."

He cups my chin and presses his forehead against mine, our faces so close our breath mingles together. "They know, Love. They know. How could they not? They were your family."

And I feel his certainty and his unconditional love. Despite my scars. Despite my past. Despite all the bad I've done. This man before me, this man who sacrificed himself for everyone, he loves me.

Warmth floods me. A craving so strong I can't stop it. I need him. Need to feel him. To touch him. To be with him.

He lets out a breath, then a moan of desire as my need washes over him. "Evangeline... "

"Ivan... "

His mouth is on mine in an instant, soft at first, then harder, the passion building. We both stand, our chairs falling behind us with our need to get closer. He pulls me toward him and lifts me into his arms. "Is this what you want?" he asks, his voice husky.

"Yes. I want you. All of you."

In a few steps we're at the bed. He lays me down and slowly pulls his shirt off, then his pants. I watch in awe, admiring the muscles, the planes, the strength in every inch of his body. He smirks at me, standing there in all his glory. "You, my love, are wearing too many clothes."

"Then you should probably take them off," I tease.

He groans and glides his hands over me, tugging at my skirt and panties, and slowly pulls them down my legs. I lift my torso so he can remove my blouse. I'm completely naked now, and his eyes feast on my body just as I do on his.

In the past, I've always insisted on darkness when with a man. I've never let anyone see the scars from my accident.

Now I have new scars mingled with the old, but rather than cover myself, I bare myself to him, heart and soul and body. We are both perfectly imperfect. Our scars tell our stories. And for the first time, I realize my scars don't make me ugly. They make me whole. They are part of who I am. It is our imperfections that make us truly beautiful.

With slow deliberation, his hands skim over my body, lingering on every curve, tracing every dip. I bite my lip to keep from moaning loudly as he settles on my breasts, using his tongue to trace their shape before sucking the peaks into his mouth one at a time, the feel of his fangs an aphrodisiac —an erotic scrape here and there. When his hand slides between my legs, I arch my hips, urging him to claim me as his, craving him more and more with each touch.

I moan and feel his smile as his lips continue to trace my skin. Every inch is worshipped, even the places I once found ugly and embarrassing. Somehow, with his touch, he heals them—not on the outside—but on the inside where it matters the most. I feel beautiful and desirable as the physical manifestation of his excitement presses against my leg.

When his mouth finally reaches mine, I trace his face with my fingers, memorizing every inch. He is gorgeous, perfect, and mine.

I can't hide my mewl of disappointment when he withdraws his hand from between my legs. Watching me, he lifts his wrist to his mouth and bites deep into the skin.

"Drink," he holds his arm out to me. I cup it with both hands and bring it to my mouth. Aroused as I am, I don't have time to think about things like blood. All I know is that

I want to taste him, to feel him, to bond with him in every way.

He groans as I drink, sucking as much as I can and letting it flow down my throat. Letting his power fill me. His pleasure is my pleasure.

"Enough," he whispers and gently extracts his arm from my grasp. Like before, I make a mewl of disappointment, and this time he chuckles before sliding his weight between my legs. "I want you, Love."

"I'm already yours, Ivan." I feel him pressing at my entrance and lift my hips.

Just like with everything else, he takes his time. With our bodies pressed against each other, so close to becoming one, I tilt my neck to the side. "Your turn," I whisper through a haze of lust and love and power.

His arousal grows as his lips brush against the sensitive skin of my neck. "You're beautiful," he whispers. "I don't deserve someone so beautiful."

His teeth graze at the pulsing vein, his tongue tracing a line of fire down my jaw.

My nails dig into his muscular back, trailing along his scars. "You're the most amazing man I've ever met. If anyone is lucky, it's me."

As his teeth sink into my neck, he drives into me, and my body electrifies by a thousand lightning bolts. Pleasure, pain, and power merge within me, forming an erotic trio that ignites every nerve in my body.

And that's when he begins to move. Slowly, achingly. He pulls away from my neck, licking the blood off his lips, his eyes aglow with everything I feel within. We hold each other's gazes, the desire becoming so intense I can barely remember who I am anymore.

My climax shatters us both, and we clutch each other as

we ride the wave together.

When we are both spent, our bodies slick with sweat, my head resting in the crook of his arm, he holds me tight and whispers into my hair. *"Ya lyublyu tebya."*

"I love you too," I sigh, holding him more tightly.

This man is mine.

And I will do anything to protect him.

CHAPTER 7: TIME TO MAKE A BITCH PAY, IF YA' CATCH MY DRIFT. ALSO, DON'T WAKE THE SLEEPING VAMPIRE, HE WON'T BE HAPPY.

I FAILED MY FAMILY.

I failed myself.

For too many years I have failed everyone around me because I wouldn't forgive myself.

I will not fail the man sleeping by my side.

I'm guessing it's mid-day, and since Ivan hasn't turned me yet, I still get to enjoy the sun. That means I can end this nightmare he's been living in for too many centuries.

He's not going to like my plan, but if it works, it will be worth it.

I just have to avoid getting killed, since that would kill him too, and I'm not going to be responsible for another death of someone I love.

The quietness of the cave settles into me as I stare into the face of the man who has stolen my heart. I brush my lips against his and whisper, "I'm going to fix this. I'll be back."

And then I dress and leave, making my way back to Vara's house through the forest and the snow. I really need my own wardrobe if I'm going to keep living here. I shiver and pull my cloak tighter around me as I approach the village.

It's a somber day with a gray sky. Almost no one is out, which makes me wonder what else happened while we were sleeping.

I come to Vara's back door, making sure to avoid detection by anyone, and knock.

She answers on the third knock. "Evangeline, come in. What are you doing here?"

I slip into the house, and she closes and locks the door behind me. "I had to speak to you," I say. "I need your help."

She frowns. "This isn't a good time."

It takes me a moment to realize her eyes are swollen and red and she looks like she hasn't slept. "What happened?" I ask.

"The creature struck again. He killed a dear friend of mine." She locks her gaze with mine. "You have not been able to kill him, I take it?"

I shake my head. "That's what I came to tell you. There's been a huge mistake. He isn't the killer you think he is."

She invites me to sit in front of her fire, and we sip on tea as I tell her everything and explain my plan. "I think Boris is controlling the Koschei. He must have found the egg that houses his soul. We have to break into Boris's house and find it, then we can stop the killings."

This, of course, is assuming the egg is in his house. But it's a small village. Where else would he keep it where he knew it would be safe?

Vara nods slowly. "This is...astonishing. How could he have kept this from us? What was he thinking?"

"Those are questions for later. Right now we need end this bloodshed. I don't think Ivan can keep this up much longer. Fighting the Koschei each night is hurting him."

"Ivan?" she says, raising an eyebrow.

"That's his name," I say, trying not to show too much emotion.

"How have you been able to speak to him?" she asks. "Has your Russian improved so much in such a short time?"

For some reason, I don't feel comfortable telling her about the bond. "Between his bits of English and my bits of Russian, we've made do," I say. "How is it you know English so well?"

"From my grandfather. He wasn't from here. He was English and stumbled upon our village by accident. Then, of course, he could never leave. He eventually fell in love with my grandmother and they made sure my mother knew both English and Russian."

I nod. "Have there been a lot of outsiders who have come here over the years?" I ask.

"More than you might expect. Unfortunate for them, but it has helped keep our gene pool diverse. And though we can't incorporate technology, we can learn about it. But I do wonder sometimes what it would be like to embrace the rest of the world." There's a longing in her eyes I've never seen before, and it makes me curious.

"If Boris controls the monster he, or someone, can kill it. That should break the curse. That should free you," I say.

She nods. "It would free all the monsters in our village."

If frown at her comment, but a wave of dizziness hits me, and I lose my train of thought. "Could I...would you mind getting me a glass of water?" I ask. "I'm not feeling well."

She smiles. "Of course. I'll be back in a moment."

While she's gone I stand, stretching my muscles and trying to rid myself of this uneasiness. Maybe it's from too much blood? Or my body is already turning? We never really talked about what that process would be.

I take the time to myself to admire the beautiful collection of art pieces in her living room and come upon a collection of painted eggs. There are five, though the center one looks different from the rest.

"Those are *pysanka*," Vara says from across the room. "A tradition in our culture."

"They're beautiful," I say, as my legs wobble beneath me. Something is very wrong. Panic surges in my gut as the pieces click together. "This middle one, why is it different?"

I hold it up, and Vara crosses the room quickly, grabbing it from me. "Do not touch it. It's very special." She cradles it like a child, and I glance over at my tea, suspicions forming as I sway and clutch the fireplace mantlepiece to avoid collapsing.

"The tea should have worked by now," she mumbles, her eyes fixated on the egg. "What has the beast in the forest done to you?"

"He's made me stronger," I say, as a surge of power pours through me. It's Ivan. Somehow he's giving me his strength. It burns away the effects of the tea, but I don't let her see this. Instead, I fall into the chair, feigning weakness I no longer feel. The truth is, I feel like I could lift a horse right now. It's heady and exhilarating.

"It was you?" I ask. "You've been controlling Koschei? That's his soul, isn't it?"

She smiles, pacing the room with her egg. "Yes. It's been me all along."

"Why? Why kill your own people? Your own friend?"

Her smile drops. "That was unfortunate, and I feel truly awful for it. But Sasha found out what I was doing and would have ruined everything. You see, I want to break the curse on this village. Boris wants us to stay trapped forever.

He believes it keeps us pure. He has to be stopped or we will never be free."

I glance outside and notice the sun setting. Ivan will awaken soon. He'll know where I am. I have to keep her talking.

"So why not break the egg if you have it. That will end it."

She shakes her head. "That will free the other monster. Ivan, as you call him. Do you think he's innocent? Ask him who he killed when he became a vampire. Ask him how many innocent lives he's taken."

"And what of you?" I ask. "How many lives have you taken for your own selfish ends?"

She just smiles. "You are too young to understand. To fully appreciate what needs to be done for the good of all, and now you will never know. That tea will end your life, but you will go peacefully. I can't say the same for the monster you've clearly bedded."

I recoil at the bitterness in her voice. She hates Ivan. Detests him.

"What did he do to you?" I ask.

She narrows her eyes at me. "He killed my only child. My son, who went into the woods at my beckoning to end the life of the monster."

"So...you sent your son to kill Ivan, and Ivan defended himself? That's tragic but also, what the hell?"

But she's no longer listening to me. She shakes the egg, whispering words in Russian, and then smiles. "It has begun. Tonight, under the full moon, when the Koschei is the strongest, and the monster in the woods is at his weakest, they will battle. Koschei will win. And then I will kill Koschei and free us all."

I'm totally expecting a *mwahaha* at the end of this, but

nope. She just closes her eyes, confident in her tea's ability to knock me out.

I need to stop her.

Need to stop Koschei before he gets too Ivan.

I look around the room and see a small pile of wooden stakes in the corner. Shit this woman is determined to end my mate's life. Not today, bitch. Not on my watch.

With speed that surprises both of us, I lunge for a stake and then slam it into her chest with a sickening crack and thud. The egg falls from her hand and topples to the floor along with her body.

With the wood sticking out of her heart, blood trickling from her mouth, she stares at me as her life seeps away.

"You will regret this," she mumbles just as her soul leaves her.

"Nope, don't think so, bitch," I say as I reach for the egg.

I'm shaking, and I can't stand to look at her too long. But I know I did the right thing. I have to save Ivan.

I throw the egg to the ground, expecting it to break, but it doesn't. I step on it, smash it, even throw it into the fire. Nothing.

Shit.

This isn't going how I planned.

I've got to get to Ivan.

Cupping the egg, I leave through the backdoor and run to the forest. Darkness has descended, but the moon lights my way. I run impossibly fast, and I hear them fighting before I see them.

Ivan is covered in blood and new gashes. Koschei is a phantom terror, a shadow dark as night, a terror made flesh. Bile burns my throat, but I swallow it and reach for Ivan with our bond.

Then I hold up the egg for him to see. But Koschei sees it too and runs towards me.

In a panic I throw the egg to Ivan as hard as I can. He catches it and using his vampire teeth he bites into the egg, cracking it open just as Koschei reaches me, his sharp claws slashing at my belly, ripping it apart.

I scream. Ivan screams.

The egg breaks.

And Koschei crumbles to the ground.

He and I lie side by side, dying, and under the rays of the full moon, his monstrous form begins to fade, revealing the man he once was.

Ivan rushes to us both, cradling me in his arms, watching his old apprentice return.

"Master," the boy whispers through blood, "I have failed you. I am sorry. Thank..." he chokes on more blood. "Thank you for ending it."

And then he dies.

Ivan looks down at me, at my stomach. "I have to turn you, Love. Right now."

I nod. I'm ready.

If I never see my family again, I will live my life here on earth making up for what I've done. Helping others through their grief.

Ivan drinks from me deeply, more deeply than he ever has before, until I'm a husk, and then he feeds me his own blood, filling me back up.

He whispers words into my ear as I fall asleep in his arms, his blood humming through me, binding us forever.

CHAPTER 8: WHERE ALL THE HAPPY SHIT HAPPENS... I DON'T WANT TO SPOIL IT, BUT DUN DUN DA DUNNNNNN...

"NOT YET!" I shout through the door with a smile as I adjust my wedding dress. It's a beautiful white gown embroidered with red in the Ukrainian style. Yana is by my side, helping.

"Stay still," my best friend says. "You're mussing your hair."

So much has happened since the night we broke the curse and Ivan turned me. Once we were able to leave the village, we went in search of the plane I was in, and found that there were survivors, including my best friend. She suffered some pretty bad injuries, but has mostly recovered, though she still limps. I filled her in on my adventures, and though she's still trying to wrap her mind around it all, she's here, supporting me in this unusual union.

When I'm finally ready, I step out of the bedroom and into the embrace of my soon-to-be husband. Yana sighs. "You're breaking all the traditions!"

I shrug. "I'm American, and he predates everything. I think we can justify a few changes."

The three of us make our way down to the village. The moon is high in the sky, and the village square is filled with candles and festive decor. A band is playing, everyone is dressed in their finest, and a feast is displayed for after the service.

The evening is a blur. We step on the *rushnyk*, an embroidered cloth that supposedly determines who will 'wear the pants' in the family, together. At the same time. It was a decision we made—that we would be equals in all things. We say our vows, there are games, activities, so many toasts I can't count, and I lose myself in the joy of seeing the people of this village embrace Ivan as one of them. They all now know what he's been doing for them these long centuries. They know of his sacrifices. I made sure of that. I also made sure Boris was removed from power and punished for his crimes against humanity.

There's one more surprise in store, and at our reception, I call for a toast. "I know this is unusual, but what part of this hasn't been?" I say in my best Russian. I've been practicing. "But I'd like to propose that Ivan become the new village elder to lead us into the future. He has certainly earned it."

There are cheers and many calls for this to be done. Ivan looks at me in shock, then smiles and pulls me into his arms. "What have I done to deserve someone like you?"

"I'm the lucky one, you fool. You saved me."

He kisses me and smiles again.

"We saved each other."

Dear Reader,

Thank you for reading *Forever Bound*, a Vampire Brides novella. There are eleven total novellas in this shared world, each of them a standalone paranormal romance. We, the

Midnight Coven authors, hope you'll check out all of them. They all share a world but can be read in any order.

For a bonus scene from *Forever Bound*, sign up for our newsletter!

———

DON'T MISS A SINGLE BRIDE!

Forever Claimed by Kim Loraine
Forever Magnolia by Dyan Chick
Forever Blood by Lisa Manifold
Forever Kept by Patricia D. Eddy
Forever Still by Corinne O'Flynn
Forever Desired by Ariel Marie
Forever Onyx by Alice K. Wayne
Forever Chosen by K.L. Bone
Forever Immortal by Amelia Hutchins
Forever Taboo by Nichole Chase
Forever Bound by Karpov Kinrade

The Midnight Coven will be back soon with our next collaboration—Vampire Mates. In the meantime, we hope you'll join our Facebook Group. We'd love to see you there!

———

SNEAK PEEK: CHAPTER ONE - FOREVER CLAIMED

Mattias

I am going to kill this man tonight. I made a promise to my clan that I'd get vengeance for the mutilation of Axel and murder of his mate, so here I am, all the way in the Pacific Northwest. I'd much rather be home in Stockholm, enjoying living a life out in the open rather than hiding my vampire nature. But it is my duty to avenge Axel's mate, Luna. I won't let him down.

Wind rustles through the leaves, and with each step on the spongy earth, dry, brittle twigs crunch under my feet. My senses are momentarily overwhelmed by the foul stench of decay from a stagnant pond nearby mixing with the wind carrying the scent of woodsmoke through the air. I force myself to control and focus my attention. I can't let the surroundings overshadow my intended target.

Three hearts beat as two other humans join my prey and they convene in the distance, their beer-soaked sweat proving exactly what I thought to be true. The man I'm looking for is off his game. Hunters are supposed to be quick, sharp, dangerous. Two of them are sloppy, and my target is already buzzed. This will be a walk in the park.

"You bring the stuff?" one man asks, his voice thin and tight. He's coming down from a high, I can sense it in the rapid beat of his pulse.

"I told you, I'm not using anymore. Strictly booze and smokes. It fucks with my brain too much. I've got a job to do."

The third guy laughs, and from what I can see through the brush, he sits on a fallen log and takes a drag on his cigarette. "I bet you still think vampires are real, don't you? Seems like your brain is already fucked. Maybe we need to lock you in the loony bin."

The hunter growls, his frustration scenting the air. "Believe what you want. I'm not going to explain my job to you again."

"Shit, man, you're no fun anymore."

I shift my position, and a fucking animal darts out from the bush in front of me. It skitters and rustles the leaves loud enough to draw attention to my location, and I do my best to sink into the darkness. The hunter looks over his shoulder in my direction, and I slink back into the shadow afforded me by the trees. They can't see me. They can't know I'm here. He may be drunk, but he's still a hunter. If I underestimate him, I'll put myself at risk.

"Come on," he says. "Let's get out of these fucking woods. See what kind of trouble we can stir up before I have to go on another job."

"Oh, I know. I've had my eye on a real pretty piece the last few weeks. Let's see if she's up for a little fun."

I don't care who said it, just that they're about to head into public view. I can't kill the hunter if he's in the middle of a city.

I could take them all down, but there's no guarantee the hunter wouldn't fight. I'm sure he's got at least one stake on him, possibly a silver blade. I need to catch him unawares, and at this point, my cover has likely been blown. He was too eager to leave. Damn.

I let them get to the edge of the woods, their disgusting, unwashed scents getting fainter by the moment. Then I follow.

He will die tonight.

Laney

"That's a sixteen-ounce caramel mocha with whip and a blueberry scone. Anything else?" I ask, handing the food and drink across the counter. The warm caramel and sweet blueberry scents tangle in the air, and I let the comfort they provide ease my tension, if only for a moment.

"I said no whip," the woman says, her face twisted into an angry scowl. "Can't you baristas get anything right?"

I cringe inwardly. The line is out the door, and I'm here all alone because my only employee is out sick—again. Murmurs of the people in line make me "I'm sorry. I'll scoop the whip off for you."

She huffs and shakes her head. "I'm going to be late as it is."

Then she turns on her heel and sashays away.

No tip.

That's how it's been all day. I've been slammed since dawn, and by the time the sun sets and time six o'clock hits, I'm exhausted. I count the register, put the deposit in the safe, and clean the shop until it gleams. When I step outside, the sky is fully dark, and the cold air of the Pacific

Northwest evening sends a chill through me. My breath fogs with every exhalation, and I shove my hands into the pockets of my wool coat, trying to keep warm. The Nordic-themed town where I live is already going quiet, the hour too early for brewery crawls and too late for small business owners to stay open. This weekend though? It'll be full of tourists hitting up the famous historic landmarks.

"Look what we have here, boys," a gravelly voice says from the alley as I pass by on the way to the parking lot up the hill.

Shit. I rifle through my purse for my pepper spray as apprehension prickles along the back of my neck.

"She's a pretty piece. I bet she's got a whole bag full of tips from that coffee shop." This guy's words are laced with a mixture of mockery and desperation.

Glancing over my shoulder, I see the two of them, dirty and probably still high from their last fix. "Leave me the fuck alone," I say, still trying to find my one weapon. But the visual of my bed where I'd left the items from my old purse before switching to a new one sends dread curling in my stomach. Shit. Shit. Shit.

"I don't think that's a good plan at all, darlin'. I think you should come over here and spend some time with us."

I keep walking, the click of my boot heels loud on the silent streets, but I'm very aware of them right behind me. Then, a third guy comes around a corner in front of me, his cap pulled low to cover his face. I'm stuck between them, the scent of stale beer and cigarettes making me nauseous. "Please, you can have my money. Just let me go." I remember clearly what my very first boss told me about shoplifters and burglaries when I was sixteen. *Give them what they want and get out of there. We have insurance; we can't get you back.*

I pull out the brown paper sack filled with my meager

tips and thrust it at the guy in front of me, but the other two are already too close for comfort. "I think we'll take more than your money. You tease us every damn day in those low-cut sweaters."

My stomach turns when I realize these are the guys who hang out on the corner most evenings. They've been watching me. Waiting for a night when I'd be alone.

"I'm not interested," I say, trying to shove past them. They grab me, all three at once, and I scream, but hands that smell of tobacco cover my mouth as they drag me toward the alley. Sticky grime pulls at my shoes, making me slip even with their hands on me. I fall hard on my knee, the cold, wet asphalt digging into my skin.

"Stand up, bitch. We need a little entertainment."

I'm wrenched to my feet, pain burning in my shoulder. I can't help but cry out as one of the guys slides in behind me and licks a line up my neck. A shudder of revulsion rolls through me, and a tear trails down my cheek.

"You'd do well to put the lady down if you'd like to keep your arms," a deep, masculine voice says, but I can't see him through the men holding me. Hope blossoms in my chest, the thought of someone here to help grabbing on and not letting go.

One of the guys releases me and walks toward the mystery man. I catch sight of my rescuer. Tall and broad, he looks like an avenging angel with his golden hair glowing like a halo in the streetlight. This man is going to save me.

"Who the fuck do you think you are?" my attacker asks him, getting closer.

"I'm the man who is going to end you here and now."

The man rushes my savior but he's thrown against the brick wall of the building next to us with such force the window above him cracks. My assailant falls, unconscious, maybe dead, and the two men still holding me let out curses. I twist and turn, desperate to get out of their grips. With everything in me, I stomp on one man's instep, and as soon as his grip loosens, I twist and free my arm, jutting the heel of my hand into the other guy's nose. They're both groaning in pain, but they release me, shove me to the ground, and run. The man who saved me doesn't go after them, instead he strides toward me, and my breath catches at the sight of his face. Chiseled to perfection with ice blue eyes, he looks like my vision of a Nordic prince.

"Th—thank you," I say, adrenaline making my words falter as my body trembles.

"Are you all right?" He holds out a hand to help me up, and I take his offering. His large palm engulfs mine, a spark passing through me at the contact.

"I am now. I'm so glad you came along."

I'm still shaking, and he hasn't released my hand. "Do you live nearby?"

"I was walking to my car." I shrug. "I'm not too far from here."

"I'll accompany you to ensure your safety."

I laugh and look up, up, up his considerable height. "God, you're tall."

He smirks, his full lips suddenly all I can focus on. "And you're tiny."

I straighten my shoulders. I am petite at 5'2". Usually that's something I don't like about myself, but the way he called me tiny makes me feel delicate in a way my curves typically don't allow. "How tall are you?"

"Six feet and five inches. That's how you Americans say it, correct?"

So I was right, he's not from around here. "Correct. Where are you from?"

"Sweden. I'm...visiting some relatives."

His pause makes me wonder what he's hiding. He's got to be a prince or something. Taking in the designer coat and scarf he's wearing along with just...everything about him, there has to be more to this man.

He releases my hand and slips out of his coat, draping it over my shoulders. Then he offers me his arm. I thread mine through the crook of his elbow, and the scents of cedar and leather overtakes my senses. Involuntarily, I draw in a long breath and savor him.

"All right?" he asks.

I've stopped shaking, and my cheeks heat with embarrassment. "You smell nice."

His eyes crinkle at the corners when he smiles. "So do you."

"I smell like coffee."

Leaning down, he brings his face close to mine and mimics my long inhalation. "No. Orchids and vanilla."

Swoon. Things low in my body tighten, and I wonder how I went from a near sexual assault to a fairy tale. "My car is just up here," I say, because if I don't change the subject, I might kiss him.

"I'm at your disposal."

We walk together in the crisp night air, silence between us, but a strange sense of comfort as well. When we reach my car, I wish I'd parked farther away. I pat the top of my beat-up old coupe, and grin. "This is me. Thank you for the rescue..." I leave my words hanging in the air, hoping he'll give me his name.

"Mattias," he says, offering me a slight bow of his head.

"I'm Laney...Elaine...but everyone calls me Laney." God, now I'm tripping over my own name.

"It was my pleasure, Elaine."

My heart swells and flutters at the sound of my full name on his lips. He leans close, his big body so near mine, caging me in without making me feel uncomfortable. Then, his lips brush my cheek and he steps away. I open my car door and look back at him as I slide into the driver's seat. "Will I see you again?"

He nods. "Without doubt."

I start the car and pull forward with the scent of him still lingering. Now, instead of dreading work tomorrow, I can't wait to come back because of the possibility of seeing Mattias again. I resist the urge to look for him, I don't want him to think I'm desperate, but I do risk a glance in the rearview mirror. Disappointment and confusion swirl in my gut. He's gone. How is that possible? I stare over my shoulder and shock rolls through me when I see him standing right where I left him, watching over me as I leave. My brow furrows, and I return my focus to the mirror. Nothing.

"What the fuck?" I whisper, but when I cast my gaze back to the place where Mattias was standing, this time he's nowhere to be found.

You've just read Chapter One of Forever Claimed by Kim Loraine.
You can find more of this story here.

ALSO BY KARPOV KINRADE

Get the soundtrack for I AM THE WILD, OF DREAMS AND DRAGONS and MOONSTONE ACADEMY wherever music can be found.

THE FORBIDDEN TRILOGY (complete sci fi thriller romance)

ABOUT THE AUTHOR

Karpov Kinrade is the pen name for the husband and wife writing duo of USA TODAY bestselling, award-winning authors Lux Karpov-Kinrade and Dmytry Karpov-Kinrade.

Together, they live in Ukiah, California and write fantasy and science fiction novels and screenplays, make music and direct movies.